Robert the Allotm

Robert The Movie Star

By Nicholas Mays

Illustrated by Rebecca Homewood

First Printing 2020

Published by Long Way Round Publishing (UK)

www.LongWayRoundPublishing.co.uk

E-mail: LongWayRoundPublishing@gmail.com

To Tom, a very brave boy and Amelia, his very smart sister

And

Rebecca and Jason, two brilliant parents

And

Rosie, Fluffy and Zoom – of course!

And

All our Healthcare Professionals, Frontline Staff and Volunteers.
You're ALL Amazing!

Robert The Movie Star

CHAPTER ONE

It's All Gone Quiet Over There

I'm Robert the Allotment cat, and I observe things.

Being a cat, I'm observant by nature of course, but when you've been an Outling Cat – that is a cat of no fixed human abode – you learn to be extra observant. You have to use all your senses. Sight obviously - if it moves, it might be dangerous, or it might be something to pounce on and eat. Or you may just need to keep an eye on whatever it is and what it's doing for future reference. Hearing is just as important as sight, it might signify danger coming your way or again, it might be something to eat. Smell too – we cats go a great deal on smell. We can detect a dog long before we see or hear it, but then dogs do have a pretty strong smell to start with, so that's not surprising. Taste – well that's obvious. If it tastes nice, you can eat it. Touch – if it feels soft, you can sleep on it. If it's wet, don't sit on it or sleep on it. Or if it's prickly, it's most likely a hedgehog and they don't like being slept on anyway. Basically, you need to keep your wits about you.

So, even though I've lived at Sunnyside Allotments in the city of Midlandtown for quite some time now, I haven't lost my Outling skills of observation. I just don't need to use them quite as much, because Betty and the plot holders are always bringing us nice things to eat and giving us nice soft beds to sleep on. It was perhaps for this reason that my Outling observational skills kicked in just recently when I noticed something very odd about the allotments and, indeed, the human plot holders. I mean, humans behave very strangely at the best of times, but… well, hang on. Let me tell you what happened. Red Fred, Dorothy and I were basking in the sun by the kale…

'Have you noticed how quiet it is?' I said, looking about me as I had a quick wash. 'It's been like that for days now.'

'Can't say as I have mate,' yawned Red Fred, stretching out his massive, marmalade body from front paws to tail tip, nudging Dorothy out of the way as he did so. He sat up and scratched his neck with one of his hind legs. 'These new collars Betty put on us can be a bit itchy at times.'

'Hmm,' said Dorothy, shooting Red Fred *a Look* for disturbing her from her nice warm patch of earth in the sunshine. 'The allotments aren't what you call the hub of all human activity at the best of times. Maybe everyone's on holiday.'

'It doesn't *feel* like a holiday,' I said. 'Holidays smell different somehow. Taste different too.'

'There's still plot holders about mate,' said Fred. 'Look, there's a couple over there.'

'But they're so far apart,' I said. 'I saw two others on their plots calling over to each other. It seemed a bit strange.'

'They *always* do that,' put in Dorothy. 'They work on their own plots and they're set apart from each other, so they have to shout across to each other.'

'True, true,' I conceded. 'But if they want to have a *conversation*, one of them will usually go over to the other one's plot. Sometimes they sit down and share a flask of tea. These two were having a conversation but calling across to each other, like they didn't want to get too close or something.'

'Humans are odd,' said Dorothy dismissively, washing between her front toes, then furiously nibbling at the dirt stuck under one of her claws.

'Rob's right though,' said Fred. 'I've seen 'em doing that too. None of 'em are going onto each other's plots to talk. And when I was in the clubhouse the other day, Betty and Colin were in there and they were standing well apart while they were talking. Betty had made 'em cups of tea in the kitchen but Colin waited 'til she'd moved away before he went to pick his mug up.'

'That's right!' I exclaimed. 'I saw that too. *And* they haven't had a Committee meeting for ages. I should know,' I added proudly. 'After all, I'm an honorary trustee *and* committee member.'

Dorothy sighed and yawned, which is quite a feat to do both at once. 'How would you know if there was a committee meeting anyway?' she scoffed. 'As soon as everyone's sat down, stroked you and given you treats you fall asleep on the table. They could be doing anything while you're snoozing your head off.'

'I *listen*,' I retorted indignantly. 'I *observe*. You don't have to have your eyes open to *observe*. And that's another thing – the traffic on the main road is really quiet. I went up to the gate yesterday and looked out and there's hardly any cars or lorries going past. Hardly any people out and about either. I don't reckon they've all gone away on holiday.'

'I haven't seen many planes going overhead either,' added Red Fred. 'It's funny, you don't notice things if they're around all the time. Then when they're not there, you *do* notice 'em. Like, *not* notice 'em, sorta fing... if you know what I mean.'

Dorothy sighed in exasperation, but I backed Fred up. 'That's right!' I said. 'Isn't Midlandtown City Airport a few miles away from here? Don't tell me nearly all the planes have gone on holiday too. Come to think of it, have you heard any noise from the stadium construction site lately?'

The stadium construction site was over the far side of the allotments. Since our adventures when we'd saved the allotments from being built on, a different company was working on the stadium and had put up a new metal fence between the allotments and the building site. They weren't as noisy or as messy as the previous lot, but even with the fence there was always the background noise of machinery. Until recently anyway.

'It's the virus.'

'What did you say?' said Dorothy, looking up sharply.

'I didn't say anything,' I said.

'Nor me,' added Fred.

'It was me,' said a shy little voice from the kale patch behind us. Janet poked her tabby head through. Even though she'd got braver lately, she still preferred to spend time over the Wild Side of the allotments, near the pond. Like the rest of us, she was wearing a new collar. Hers was pink, I noticed, although mine was black, like my fur. They were very smart for flea collars, I thought.

'Oh, it's Thingy,' said Dorothy dismissively, continuing to wash her paws. 'What would *you* know anyway? You're never around this end.'

I ignored Dorothy's snootiness and tried to encourage Janet to stay. 'Never mind her, *Janet,*' I said, deliberately emphasising her name for Dorothy's benefit. 'Tell us what you know.'

'Well…' said Janet hesitantly. 'I heard some of the men on the construction site talking the other day – just before they all stopped work and went away. And then I heard two plot holders shouting about it to each other. There's something called a *virus* going around the humans – it's an illness – and it's very catching, Apparently, humans have to stay indoors and not go out unless it's really necessary. And if they *are* outdoors, they mustn't stand too close together in case one of them has the virus and passes it to the other one. It… it… well, it sounds like cat flu and we all know how awful *that* can be.'

We must have all looked shocked. Even Dorothy seemed taken aback at this. Typically though, it was Dorothy who took a decision. 'We need to find out more about this,' she said decisively. 'Robert, Fred, Jammy – go and round up the Usual Suspects. I think it's time we took a look at Betty's laptop!'

CHAPTER TWO

Logging On

It was later that afternoon when all six of us Allotment cats were gathered behind one of the sheds nearest the clubhouse. It was around this time of day that Betty usually left in her car for an hour or so – we guessed to go home for her tea - then came back to lock up the clubhouse and gate. There were only a couple of other plotholders around and they were working near the centre of the allotments on their separate plots, so nobody else was near the clubhouse.

'Ah, here she comes,' said Barbara as he peeped round the side of the shed. 'Go and do your thing, Robert. Make sure she doesn't suspect anything.'

I trotted over to Betty as she exited the clubhouse carrying her car keys. I noticed that, unusually, Betty's face was set in a tight frown, making her look very serious. 'Hello Betty!' I said, flopping down on the paved area outside the clubhouse and rolling over. (Of course, Betty would have only heard me say "*Miaow*", but sometimes I think she understands a lot of what I say, more than most humans can).

'Oh, hello Robert,' she said, a smile breaking out on her face and dispelling the frown as she bent down to tickle my tummy. 'I suppose you'd like some cat treats, would you?' I purred in reply which, as always, made her chuckle. As usual, she was wearing her green sleeveless anorak with the multiple pockets. And, as usual, she rummaged in one of those pockets and produced a few cat treats which she dropped down for me. I quickly started eating them, purring happily. 'I'll be back to give you your supper later,' she added conversationally. 'The clubhouse is open if you want to go in. I'm going to try to get some shopping… assuming the queues aren't too bad!' With that she unlocked the door to her car which was parked nearby, muttering to herself as she threw a bundle of gardening catalogues off the dashboard onto the passenger seat. She hopped in and started the engine. I noticed that the frown was back on her face.

As I watched her drive away, the other cats slipped out from behind the shed and hurried over. I thought their new collars suited them. Pink for the girls, blue for the boys. I was quite proud of my black one – it made me feel a bit special.

'Didn't leave us any treats, did you?' grumbled Dorothy.

'E-e-everything *okayRobert*? Y-y-y-you look *abitconcerned*.'' wibbled E.T., as she crab-walked up to me in her usual wobbly way. (E.T. suffers from a condition that's got a really complicated name, but everybody knows it as Wobbly Cat Syndrome. It doesn't bother E.T., nor the rest of us cats. It's just the way she is. Anyway, she's got a magnificent fluffy tail and her white coat is always spotlessly clean. Her name seems to amuse humans for some reason, but who cares? After all, Barbara is a boy and apparently Barbara is a girl's name in Humanese, but he knows who he is and so do we. Humans can't smell or taste our real cat names anyway).

'Oh, I'm okay thanks E.T.,' I replied. 'I just thought Betty looked a bit, well, *worried*. I reckon it must be this virus thing that's bothering her.'

'Not surprising really,' said Gloria Glover (we call her G.G.). 'A lot of the plot holders look miserable. I think they're lonely as well as worried. Some of the older ones haven't even been to the allotments for ages. I saw Kate digging and weeding one old human's plot the other day, then she went and planted some seeds on somebody else's plot. I suppose she must be helping them out.'

'Let's hope it's not more serious than that,' added Barbara. 'It's horrible when one of those kind humans dies.'

We all fell silent for a moment, thinking of a couple of plot holders who had died in the past few months. They had both been very kind to us cats, and even though they grumbled about the birds trying to peck at their plants and eat their seeds, they'd never tried to hurt them in any way. The worst they'd do was to put up a scarecrow or clap their hands loudly when any birds landed on their plots. My friend Henry the crow just used to land on their plots for a laugh, standing there, daring them to come close before cawing loudly and then flying off. I knew even he missed the plot holders.

Dorothy brought us all back to the task in paw. 'Come on, you lot,' she said briskly. 'Let's get a look at the Interweb thingy and see what's going on.'

We cautiously crept in through the open clubhouse door, just in case there were any plot holders around having a cup of tea. Of course, they'd welcome us, but we didn't want them to know we could work the laptop. Or read and type, come to that. (Well… Dorothy and G.G. can anyway). We needn't have worried, because the clubhouse was empty.

I stopped abruptly and Dorothy cannoned into me, followed by Barbara and Red Fred, sending us sprawling. The others managed to sidestep us. 'What's up?' hissed Dorothy crossly, as she sat up and smoothed her fur down.

'What about the See Mee Pee?' I whispered back, nodding to the camera set in the corner of the wall overlooking the long table where the committee usually sat. 'They'll see what we're up to if they play the film back! Our secret will be out and – and – well, I don't know what'll happen but…'

'Oh hush!' snapped Dorothy. 'First of all, it's *CCTV*. Secondly, Betty's moved her desk and laptop over to the other side of the clubhouse, see? It's out of range of the *CCTV* camera.'

'Oh. Right. That's convenient.' I said, following her gaze to where Betty's desk now stood. Her laptop was sitting on the desk, plugged in. 'She's even left the lid up,' I added. (Betty could be quite forgetful at times). 'That's convenient too!'

'Yeah, what are the odds?' said Red Fred, drolly.

Somehow, we all managed to get up onto Betty's desk (E.T. fell off twice) and crowded around the laptop. G.G. is the only one of us who can read *and* type fast, although Dorothy can read and is learning to type whenever she gets the chance. I'm still learning to read Humanese. It's quite hard just using your eyes and not smell and taste. (I don't know how humans cope in the world, I really don't).

G.G. flexed her toes, extended her claws and tapped away at the keys to "log us on" as she said. (As usual, she stuck her tongue out of the side of her mouth as she concentrated on typing, which I always thought looked really cute, but I didn't have the courage to tell her).The screen flickered into life and G.G. opened up the Interweb thing and typed "News" into the search bar. Lots of words appeared on the screen, along with film of serious looking people in suits talking to the camera, followed by photographs of people in blue and green outfits with some kind of mask thing over their noses and mouths. Some more film showed city streets nearly empty of people and traffic. The few people that were on the streets were walking far apart from each other and some were wearing the odd face masks.

'Oh dear,' whispered G.G., almost to herself. 'That's not good at all.'

Dorothy pressed her face up to the screen and read the words too. 'Oh my,' she said, with none of her usual bravado. 'Now that *is* worrying!'

CHAPTER THREE

"Don't Call Me Dumpling!"

It all made very worrying reading indeed. Dorothy and GG read out loud to the rest of us about how an awful virus called Covid -19 had spread across the world in just a couple of months, infecting hundreds of thousands of humans and causing the deaths of many thousand too. Human doctors, nurses and other caring people (just like at the vets but for humans, as Dorothy explained) were working very hard to look after people who were badly affected.

The top humans in most places around the world had told other humans to stay at home and even work from home if they could. People could only go out if they had to buy food or go to the doctors, or if they really had to go to work, and even then, they had to stand or walk a few cat lengths apart. It was the same here in the Yoo-Kay. Dorothy told us that this rule was called a Lockdown.

'I thought that was where people kept stuff, like,' said Red Fred. 'Just like in those garages round the back of the allotments.'

Dorothy sighed and gave him one of her special Exasperated Looks. 'That's a *"lock up*, not a *"lock down,"'* she sighed impatiently. 'And before you ask, when Betty comes to lock up the clubhouse and allotments that's something else as well.'

Fred shrugged. 'Humans are weird,' he said. 'They use strange words. It's easier to talk Kittish.'

'I agree Fred,' I said, with feeling. It was all getting very confusing.

By now, Barbara and Janet had hopped onto one of the long tables which ran along the back wall of the clubhouse. As usual there were leaflets and seed packets, planting trays and all sorts of human bits and pieces, together with a small pile of…

'Your book, Robert!' exclaimed Janet excitedly. (I heard Dorothy give a dismissive snort from the desk).

'Yeah, it is,' said Barbara. He peered at the front cover of one of the books, which had a very nice drawing of me and the allotments on the front and a very fine photograph of the real me on the back. 'It says… Rob… ert… Robert…the… All…Allo…' mumbled Barbara trying to piece together the human words. (He couldn't read Humanese as well as Dorothy and G.G.).

'It says *"Robert the Allotment Cat and Friends"!'* I said proudly. 'It's the story of how I came to the Allotments and how we all saved them from being built on by that horrible landlord.'

'Of course,' said Janet. 'I've been meaning to ask though, Robert. That human that wrote it – you know, the one without any hair? How did he translate what you said into Humanese? Can he speak Kittish?'

'Ah, I'm glad you asked that,' I said, 'What happened was...'

'Never mind that silly book now!' interrupted Dorothy impatiently. 'We've just gone onto your *Facey Friends* and *Nitter-Natter* pages Robert. It looks like Betty's been posting more photos of us and writing things like you've said them and…'

Suddenly G.G. laughed out loud then slapped a paw over her mouth to stop her giggles. If something is funny enough to make a cat laugh, it must be good.

'What's so funny?' snapped Dorothy, who never likes being interrupted when she's talking. Or ever, really. G.G. simply pointed her other paw to the screen and then fell over backwards, laughing uncontrollably. Impatiently, Dorothy pushed her aside and looked closely at the screen. Suddenly her fur bristled, and she arched her back, turned around and gave me the most Withering of All Looks. 'You… called… me… "*Dorothy Dumpling*"!' she hissed angrily. 'How *dare* you?!' She swiped at me with her right paw, but I leaned back on my haunches and held my front paws out to fend her off (This is known as the *Meerkat Manoeuvre*, although I have no idea what type of cat a Meerkat is). The other cats by now were all rolling on their backs with their legs in the air laughing helplessly. E.T. had rolled right off the desk and was whiffle-laughing from Betty's chair which she had landed on.

'Whoa! *Whoa*! *I* didn't say that!' I said, trying hard not to laugh myself. 'And how could I type it? *Betty* must've said that!'

'Robert's right,' giggled G.G. sitting up again. When she realised that Dorothy was glaring at her she quickly added: 'And *I* didn't type it either!'

'Well you can all shut up!' snapped Dorothy. 'I am *not* a figure of fun!'

'Don't mention *"figure"*, Princess,' guffawed Red Fred and leapt away as Dorothy darted forward to bop him one.

'You *do* look very round in this photo,' said Janet. 'But you look as gorgeous as ever, really.'

'I have no words! You're all idiots,' snapped Dorothy jumping onto the floor and stalking away towards the door. She turned to look at us and added: 'And with that nasty virus going on, you should all be ashamed of yourselves!' With that she left the clubhouse, her tail and nose in the air.

We all fell silent.

'Oops,' I said, quietly.

A little later Red Fred, G.G. and I found Dorothy sitting in her cat bed in one of the sheds. By the time we'd all pushed in through the cat flap, Dorothy had turned her back on us. Her tail was tucked under her, but I could just see the tip poking out from under her tummy and it was twitching madly. Dorothy could even lie down angrily.

'Dorothy?' I said quietly. 'Dorothy… we're sorry. We didn't mean to make fun of you, really.'

Fred and G.G. added their apologies, along with those of Barbara, E.T. and Janet (all of whom had thought we were the best three to handle Dorothy). It took a lot of apologising until Dorothy's tail tip stopped quivering and her rigid body relaxed. She turned around slowly to face us, still giving us all a Withering Look.

'You were right Dorothy,' I said placatingly. 'Things are serious for everybody right now. Not just the humans. G.G. told us that pets are affected by the virus too.'

'Not *in*fected,' added G.G. hastily. 'Animals can't really catch it from humans. What Robert means is the lockdown and people being ill with the virus *affects* animals too. Think of the pets who have lost their owners because of this. And what if any of our plot holders got sick with it?'

'I know,' said Dorothy sulkily. 'That's why I said you should all be ashamed of yourselves.'

'Look Princess… I mean Dorothy,' said Fred, hastily correcting himself as Dorothy's Withering Look was directed towards him. 'You're right of course but, but… you've got to laugh when things are serious. It cheers you up.'

'That's right,' added G.G. 'On Robert's *Facey Friend* and *Nitter-Natter* pages, the photos of Robert – and of the rest of us, *you* especially, are cheering people up. Other humans are adding photos of their cats and dogs and other pets online and telling funny stories about them. They're even posting little films of their pets that they take with their mobile phones. Betty's done films of us too. So, you see, we *are* doing some good, we're making people *happy.*'

'I just wish we could do more,' I sighed. 'Maybe you and G.G. could type some real messages from me like we did before and…'

'That's it!' said Dorothy suddenly. 'G.G. – you said people are putting films of their cats online. *That's* what we should do! *We* should make our *own* films!'

We all looked at each other with amazement. Then we all told Dorothy what a great idea it was. Just in case.

'But hang on,' I said cautiously. 'We haven't got any mobile phones to film ourselves on...'

'*Phones*?' scoffed Dorothy. 'Where we're going, we don't *need* phones!'

CHAPTER FOUR

Movie Magic!

'I still don't get it,' I said, as we followed Dorothy back to the clubhouse. We'd rounded the other up on the way and they were just as confused as Fred, G.G. and me, although grateful that Dorothy seemed to have forgotten all about being cross with us.

'Look, it's simple,' sighed Dorothy with exasperation as we all gathered around her in the clubhouse, which was still empty of humans. 'We use the camera collars to film ourselves!' I must have looked blank because she added impatiently; '*You know* Robert – the ones that Betty and the plot holders were talking about at their last committee meeting before this lockdown came along.'

'Oh – er – yes. Remind me. For the others' benefit,' I added, rather sheepishly.

'Bah!' retorted Dorothy. ''You don't remember because you were *asleep*, weren't you? Your ears must've been "observing" something elsewhere, like your eyes. Well, I might not be an honorary committee member or a trustee, but *I* was there and *I* was listening!'

'C-c-can you *telluswha*t it's a-a about, then?' wibbled E.T.

'Yeah, preferably while it's still daylight,' put in Barbara, sarcastically.

Dorothy ignored Barbara's sarcasm. 'Right, well… Betty was telling the other committee member that she had been approached by some TV people to make a dockymenturry about us Allotment Cats. She said they were going to film us over a few days but that we cats would do most of the filming ourselves. They had special collars for us to wear with little cameras on them. They call it *KittyKam*™. The cameras can film in daylight and at nighttime.'

'Oooh!' we all chorused. This *did* sound interesting!

'Betty had been given the collars to put on us so as to get us used to wearing them, so that's why we all got new collars. Now, the TV people were supposed to be filming on the allotments about now I think, but because of this horrible virus and the lockdown I expect they're having to wait.'

'Hang on,' said Red Fred slowly. 'That little bumpy bit on the front of my collar is a camera? Doe that mean I've been filming things with this collar all this time?'

'No, you haven't,' said Dorothy. 'They haven't been switched on yet. Betty was given a little control thingy. It looks like one of those memory stick things she plugs into her laptop. And that's how they get the film of what we see onto their compyewters. She put me on the desk, held that stick thing towards me and a light came on. Then she gave me some treats. Then she put the stick thing in the side of her laptop and looked at the screen. And I saw that the screen showed the treats on the des being eaten – just how I'd just seen them! I'd made a film!'

'That's amazing!' gasped G.G. 'Let me see if that memory stick-control thingy is still in Betty's laptop.' She jumped up onto Betty's desk and checked the side of the laptop. 'It is!' she said excitedly as she jumped down to join us. 'I think I know what happens with the films Dorothy. You can upload them to files on the laptop and then put them on *Nitter-Natter* and *FaceyFriend!*' G.G. is probably the cleverest cat among us, although I wouldn't dream of telling Dorothy that. She had worked out Dorothy's plan.

Dorothy gave her a big grin. 'That's right, G.G.,' she beamed. 'I've been having a little look on the laptop the past couple of days when Betty's not been around and I've looked up information on how to make a film. If you have a look too it tells you how you can fix the film to look good. Eddying it, I think it's called. You're the best typer with the keyboard – could you do that for me when we've got some films?'

G.G. said that she could.

'So… we can use these films to cheer people up!' I exclaimed. 'That's a *great* idea, Dorothy! And we can cheer their pets up too!' The others all agreed excitedly. Dorothy held up a paw for silence.

'We're not just making silly *films*,' said Dorothy. 'Really *good* films are called *movies*, because they move so well. And they tell a proper story. Humans go to see them in special places called Sinnymars. And they watch them on TV. And on their laptops and phones. So, we're going to make movies!'

We all began to talk excitedly about what we'd like to film. Dorothy held her paw up again and we all stopped talking.

'We can't just film things willy-nilly,' she said. 'We have to have *structure*. We have to have a *plot*…'

'Loads of plots on the allotments, Princess,' put in Fred.

'Not *that* sort of plot,' sighed Dorothy impatiently. 'A movie plot is like a story. You have lines to say – that's words to make people believe that it's real. But humans can't understand what we animals say, so we won't need many lines for the actors to say. Actors are the ones in movies who speak the lines and do the actions that are filmed see? Anyway, the whole thing is controlled by the top person in charge of making the movie: The Director.'

I'd been struggling to follow all that Dorothy was saying, but I had to ask, even though I'd guessed the answer: 'Who's going to be the Director, then?'

Dorothy looked at me as though she couldn't believe I'd been silly enough to ask the question. 'The Director?' she said, with surprise. 'Why *me* of course!'

Over the next few days, Dorothy took charge of getting the film under way, along with G.G. as her assistant. Apparently, according to the information about making movies, you needed a thing called a *script*, which was lots of words written down on paper telling the story. But that was a human thing, so Dorothy and G.G. decided we didn't need that, they'd keep the story in their heads and tell us what needed to be done.

They came up with what Dorothy called "*A Thrilling Story of Feline Courage and Determination*". Basically, the story was that the allotments were under attack by an army of desperate Outling Cats who wanted to take them over. However, the Allotment Cats and other animals successfully repelled the invasion. It was a "re-imagining" of the events of the real Battle of the Allotments, when all the allotment animals had united to defend the allotments from humans employed by the evil landlord, who were going to burn them down. As we couldn't get any humans to pretend to attack the allotments, Dorothy decided it should be Outling Cats. (Quick explanation here: Home Cats are cats that choose to live with human beings. Outling Cats are cats with no human attachment who live as best they can away from humans).

This is where Dorothy's idea hit a snag. Although some of the other animals on the allotments (mainly the ones we didn't try to eat) were happy to be in the movie when we asked them, there weren't enough of us cats to make up an army of Outling Cats as well as the Allotment Cat defenders.

'We could always roll in the dirt and change our coat colours,' suggested Janet.

'Too much faffing around with multiple p.o.v. shots of you as Outling Cats and then for you to wash yourselves and become Allotment Cats,' said Dorothy.

'That's right,' agreed G.G. 'Too many separate takes to splice together.'

(I gave up trying to understand what they were both talking about at this point).

'I've got a sister called Ginger who lives across the main road,' said Red Fred casually. 'She's a sort-of Home Cat these days, but if I asked her, she could round up a few Home Cats who could pretend to be Outling Cats.'

'I didn't know you had a sister, Fred,' said Janet. 'What a coincidence.'

'Didn't think of it until just now,' said Red Fred. 'She was born on the allotments like me but set off on her own. She lives with two or three human families on the other side of the main road. She drops by the main gate every so often to say hello when she can run across the main road without getting run over. But it'd be a lot easier for her and her mates to get over the road now there's hardly any traffic.'

We all agreed this was a good idea, just as long as the Home Cats realised that this was all pretend and this didn't mean they could come to live on the allotments. Fred assured us they wouldn't think that, because they liked their home comforts too much. So we left it to Fred and Ginger to organise their troupe.

Dorothy said the movie had officially been green-lighted. I looked at the solar lights strung round the front of the club house. There were definitely green ones there, as well as red, blue, pink and yellow ones. I guessed the green ones did something special. It was all very confusing.

This movie business sounded like La La Land to me…

CHAPTER FIVE

First Day On Set

After a few practice runs with the KittyKam™ collars, Dorothy decided which of us Allotment Cats would be best to film the various parts of her movie and who had The Right Stuff to act in it. Ironically, E.T. turned out to be the best at filming, although one of us had to hold her body still while she turned her head to follow the movements of whatever she was filming. Dorothy proclaimed that she herself would also play a leading role in the film. When asked innocently by Janet whether that would be a bit much for one cat to do, Dorothy indignantly replied that *really good* Directors could Direct *and* Act, as well as write their own script.

Eventually, the first day of filming was soon upon us. Dorothy decided to make it a weekday. The lockdown was still in force; if anything, there were far less humans around both inside and outside the allotments. So that morning it was all very strange and eerily quiet.

Well, not *that* quiet really because Dorothy was shouting at everyone to stand or move or do things exactly where and how she said. E.T., Red Fred and I were on standby to film the action and do some acting ourselves. G.G. had managed to wiggle the memory-KittyKam™ control-stick thing out of Betty's laptop and had brought it out to the allotments with her. Because she had the best paws and claws for typing and pressing buttons, she was working it for Dorothy. (It was quite clever how she did this, but I can't really describe it. G.G. said it was a movie- maker's secret).

Dorothy had decided to film the big, climactic fight scene first, for no other reason it seemed than that it was more interesting than all the bits before and after. She insisted it was the artistically correct way to do it though, because all good movie makers would shoot movies "out of sequence". I said that shooting sounded a bit harsh on the movies to my mind, but after receiving a Withering Look from Dorothy, she explained that it was a Movie Term. Apparently "shooting" a movie meant the same as "filming" it.

'Well, why didn't you say "film it" instead, Smartypants?' I thought (but didn't say). I also thought (but didn't say) that I thought Dorothy had bitten off more than she could chew by having all the "extras" as she called them on the allotments on the first day. This meant that as well as all the Home Cats pretending to be Outling Cats, there were stoats, weasels, badgers, a handful of rabbits and hares and a hodgepodge of Hedgehogs all crowding around the area called 'The Set' (which only confused the badgers who started to dig holes until Dorothy yelled that 'Set' was a Movie Term and wasn't the same as a badger *sett)*.

Red Fred's sister Ginger was as Big as her brother and spoke with the same *"Ow roight mate?"* accent and equally as good natured. She'd brought about twenty Home Cats over the main road in groups of five to the allotments. Thankfully, there were few cars about, but they had to be careful all the same. They were now at the secluded area in which Dorothy had chosen to film the battle scene, milling around somewhat aimlessly. Barbara and Janet had been put in charge of taking their names and bringing them over to Dorothy to see who could act best, or *Audition* as she called it.

'How many Siamese are there?' Dorothy muttered to Barbara as she regarded a Seal Point Siamese waiting to be auditioned.

'Erm… there's three Seal Point Siamese and one Red Point,' said Barbara. 'Two of the Seal Points are sisters - the Grady Twins - if that helps.'

'Thank goodness for that,' said Dorothy. 'I was sure I'd just counted the Seventh Seal.'

'Next actor!' called G.G. 'Send over the next actor!'

'Dammit, Janet!' shouted Dorothy. 'Let the Right One In!'

'Sorry! Sorry!' apologised a harassed looking Janet as she led over an imposing Persian fellow, with lustrous long blue-grey fur. 'It's like herding humans.'

'They call me Mister Tibbs,' said the Persian, in a melodious voice. 'I've acted before. You may have seen my most recent commercial: "*FeliFood – Posh Nosh for Pedigree Pets*".' He looked around himself, rather disdainfully. 'I must say, it was a bit more organised than *this*. It's all *rather* amateurish, I must say.'

'Well, we're *trying* to get things organised!' snapped Dorothy. 'If it's not professional enough for you… well… just *bog off*!'

'Are you talking to me?' responded Mr Tibbs, arching his back and bristling. 'Well, I'm the only one here, so you must be talking to me!'

Dorothy arched her back and bristled in return, looking even more frightening. 'Go ahead, make my day!' she snarled.

'I'd watch out if I were you,' I quickly interjected to Mr Tibbs. I bent over and whispered urgently in his ear: 'I've got a bad feeling about this! She's a Wild One, she is! You wouldn't come out of it well.'

Thankfully, the film savvy fellow saw sense and backed down. 'You're a Psycho!' he retorted to Dorothy as he stalked away.

'Get off my set! You're not going to be in *my* film!' shouted Dorothy after him.

'Frankly my dear, I don't give a damn!' retorted Mr Tibbs. 'Good luck working with the Great Dictator!' he added to the next hopeful cat to present himself; a keen, wiry looking sandy-coloured chap with a cleft chin.

'I hope you can Let Me In,' he said to Dorothy.

'That depends on how well you can act,' sighed Dorothy. 'Well – what's your name?'

'I'm Spartacus!' said the cleft-chinned one helpfully.

'*I'm* Spartacus!' shouted a black and white cat sitting a few feet away.

'No, *I'm* Spartacus!' shouted the Red Point Siamese.

'Look, go away and work out which one of you is Spartacus,' growled Dorothy menacingly.

Thankfully, the wiry fellow took the hint. He narrowed his eyes and leaned forward. 'I'll be back,' he said, then set off to dispute with the other Spartacuses (Spartacii?) who was who.

'I say, Dorothy old thing, have you got a mo'?' called a familiar vixen voice. It was Ruby, one of the foxes from the wild , uncultivated part of the allotment land. I watched with interest as Ruby trotted over to Director Dorothy followed by three bouncing, bounding, giggling fox cubs. 'You and G.G. are the Producers aren't you?' she asked.

'Yes, yes, we are. We're not quite ready for you in the battle scene yet though,' said Dorothy with some exasperation.

'Not a problem old thing,' said Ruby amiably. 'I just wondered if the kids could be in the movie, what? It'd keep 'em out of mischief.'

G.G. conferred with Dorothy: 'Do you reckon we can film The Little Foxes?'

'Probably, if they do as they're told and follow my direction,' answered Dorothy, before turning around and yelling 'Will you stoats and weasels just *calm down?!* We're not doing the fight scene yet!'

'Jolly good. I can see you're busy. We'll pop orf for a while 'til you're ready for us,' chuckled Ruby. 'C'mon kidlets, come and say hello to Uncle Robert. He's a very famous cat, he is.'

The fox cubs bounded over to me, knocking me onto my back, licking me madly and yapping *'Hello Unca' Robwert!'* Somehow, I managed to struggle to my feet and maintain some sense of feline dignity. They were quite cute, but a bit too similar to small, yappy dogs for my liking. I've got History with small, yappy dogs. I smiled at them awkwardly.

'I say Robert old stick, it's quite an Animal House here, isn't it?' Ruby chuckled, before she led the cubs away, giving me a conspiratorial wink as she did so.

'Fred and Ginger!' shouted Dorothy indicating the stoats and weasels who were now squaring up to some bad-tempered hedgehogs who didn't like daylight working. 'Can you go and sort that Wild Bunch out, please?'

'Yeah, sure, Babe,' drawled Fred in his usual Carefree way. 'They're just a bit excitable. They're Goodfellas really.'

Two cats bounded up to Dorothy, cavorting and prancing like a pair of acrobats… or acrocats in this case.

'Fluffy and Zoom at your service!' they both chorused in unison. 'If you need great movers, just hire us!'

'That's *all* I need,' groaned Dorothy. 'A pair of clowns! Go and do your act over there,' she indicated a tree in the distance. 'Just as long as you're not messing up my movie.'

'Righty-ho!' Fluffy and Zoom said cheerfully, clearly oblivious to Dorothy's harsh critique of their skills. They rolled, bounced and cavorted away. It didn't help that the stoats and weasels started cheering and asking them to perform more tricks.

It was quite clear that the whole thing was getting out of paw and Dorothy was close to losing her temper completely. It was also coming up to High Noon and the sun was beating down, so taking both points into account, I decided to go for a nice, long doze under some bushes. Just as I was leaving, I saw Barbara make a potentially fatal error of judgement.

'Oh Dorothy,' he chuckled. 'You're hopping about like a Cat On A Hot Tin Roof. You're really funny.'

'What do you mean, I'm *funny?*' snapped Dorothy. 'What do you mean, the way I talk? *What?*'

Barbara began to edge away, nervously, as everyone else began to fall quiet. Even the stoats and weasels stopped jabbering and squirming and craned their long necks to see what was going on. The hedgehogs rolled up into spiky balls, because they knew what Dorothy could be like. I *definitely* knew what Dorothy could be like, so I hurried off towards the bushes.

Barbara stammered, 'It's just, you know… You're just funny, it's... funny…'

E.T hurried over from where she had been watching and interjected; 'Dorothy no, you've got *itallwrong…*'

'E.T, go home' snorted Dorothy. 'He's a big boy, he knows what he said.' She stared fixedly at Barbara. 'What did you say? Funny how? Let me understand this because, you know, maybe it's me, I'm a little messed up maybe, but I'm funny how? I mean funny like I'm a clown, I amuse you? I make you laugh? I'm here to amuse you? What do you mean funny, *funny how*? *How am I funny?*'

Barbara took the hint and fled. He came barrelling past me to escape the wrath of the Director. He was good at Silent Running and was soon Gone With The Wind.

'I'm mad as hell and I'm not going to take this anymore!' came Dorothy's hysterical howl.

I left them all to it. 'Oh well… Nobody's perfect,' I thought, as I headed off for The Big Sleep.

CHAPTER SIX

Lights! Camera! Er… Action?

I reckon it was a couple of hours later when I woke up and strolled back onto set. Things had quietened down somewhat and Dorothy was a lot calmer, although I could see how fast her tail was twitching, so her temper was likely to break at any moment if anyone said the wrong thing. The animals were sitting in various groups. I noticed that some of the Home Cats had wandered off back home, but there were still just over a dozen of them left. I noticed that the three Spartacii were sitting eagerly at the front of the group, clearly looking to be the leaders of the planned charge. The stoats and weasels were all clumped together in a heap, their sinewy bodies seeming interlocked like some fiendishly difficult puzzle. Every now and again a thin, pointy head with beady eyes, atop a long neck would pop up like a periscope to see what was happening and then disappear back down into the heap.

A few hedgehogs were still there but rolled up into balls and were most likely asleep. Ruby was sitting under a tree enjoying the shade, her cubs finally having exhausted themselves and fallen asleep. The three badgers were sitting nearby, eyeing the stoats and weasels suspiciously.

'Oh, *there* you are, Sleeping Beauty!' snapped Dorothy as I sat down next to ET who wibbled a friendly greeting. 'I was just telling everyone how the fight scene is going to go…'

Suddenly there was an excited yapping, which caused everybody to look up in surprise. That moment, a small, light brown fluffy dog came barrelling up, causing some of the Home Cats to bristle and spit angrily. We Allotment Cats didn't react like that though, because we knew who this little dog was, having got to know her over the past few months.

'Hello Rosie,' I purred, trotting over and rubbing my face against hers.

'Wotcher Robert!' yapped Rosie, giving me a swift lick on both cheeks. "Whatcha doin'? Can I join in? Why are there so many animals here? Is it a game? Can I play?' She dropped onto her belly, panting with excitement.

Now, I know what you're thinking: *But Robert doesn't like small yappy dogs!* Well, that's true, but Rosie's the exception. She's yappy for sure, but she also knows her place; she learned this the first time she came to the allotments and tried to play chase with Dorothy. Her excuse was she "did this with the cat who lived with her and her humans and the cat didn't mind because it was only play chase. Well, she didn't mind much anyway. Not all the time." Rosie belongs to a human family who have recently rented a plot at Sunnyside Allotments, apparently after reading about it in my book!

There are two grown up humans and two smaller kiddy humans, a girl and a boy. The boy is called Tom and Rosie belongs to him (dogs, of course, like to belong to humans. Us cats have a different view on that sort of thing). The girl is called Amelia and is slightly older than her brother Tom. Since the Lockdown, the grown-up humans had been taking it in turns to come to the allotments, but the children hadn't. However, Rosie would accompany them on most occasions, so I guessed one of them was tending to their plot today.

'Oh no! Mad Dog Time!' hissed Dorothy, menacingly. Before Dorothy erupted again, I quickly explained to Rosie about the film and why we were making it.

'Ooh! Can I be in it? *Please? Please?* I'll do as I'm told and everything!' Rosie babbled excitedly, literally bouncing up and down on her hind legs.

'Performing poodle or what?' I heard one of the Home Cats mutter to another, disdainfully. I turned round and gave him a Look. He quickly started to have a wash, pretending he hadn't seen me. I kept the stare up for a few more seconds then turned back to Rosie, who was still yapping.

'I know Tom would like it 'cos he's in hospital and he can't have many visitors and a film would be great 'cos he likes the allotments and the cats and all the other animals and flowers and everything and if I was in it he'd like it even more and…'

I held up a paw. 'Shhh! Rosie, shhh!' I said calmly and she flopped down again, panting, her long pink tongue hanging out of her mouth and jerking up and down like it was on elastic. 'What's this about Tom being in hospital?' A sudden, terrible thought struck me. 'He's not got that horrible virus, has he?'

'No, no, it's something else. He often has to go into hospital for a couple of weeks at a time for treatment,' said Rosie. 'I do miss him when he's away. But I can't go and visit him now 'cos of the virus thing and nor can Amelia and his mum and dad have to be so careful when they visit him and they have to wear those masks and so do all the doctors and nurses and it's not much fun for all the human kiddies in the Children's Ward.' Rosie stopped suddenly to catch her breath and pant. You have to listen fast to keep up with Rosie.

'Well, I think you should be in the movie,' I said decisively, looking at Dorothy who had been half listening. 'After all, that's why we're doing the movie, isn't it, to cheer people up?'

'I agree Chief,' said G.G., who always knows how to butter Dorothy up by flattering her. 'It'd be a great directorial decision to have a dog in the movie. Humans like dogs in movies! And it'd be great for A Boy and His Dog.'

'Yeah, and Rosie's an Allotment Dog,' I added. 'I mean, she's almost an honorary Cat.'

'That's right! She could pretend she's a Stray Dog, like those mutts up at the Reservoir,' added G.G., referring to a place that I knew all too well from my time as an Outling Cat. This was a disused reservoir controlled by a whole pack of bad tempered, half-starving stray dogs. I had always been careful to avoid even walking On the Waterfront. 'Not that we want any Reservoir Dogs in the film of course,' added G.G. quickly.

'Okay, Okay, she can be in the film!' sighed Dorothy. '*But…!*' she held up a paw just as Rosie was about to run over to her and lick her. Rosie sat. She remembered that Dorothy didn't like that sort of thing. 'But… you do as *I* tell you, understand?'

'*Ohyesohyesohyes! Thankyouthankyouthankyou Dorothy*!' yapped Rosie, her tail wagging and beating against the ground in a rapid drumbeat which caused three weasel heads to poke up in alarm.

'Call me Chief. I'm the Director,' said Dorothy grandly.

'Okay, Chief I'm the Director!' yapped Rosie, obligingly.

I had to turn away in case Dorothy saw me laughing…

Finally, Dorothy had everyone placed where she wanted them. I must admit, she'd actually done a good job of this (with help from G.G. of course). The Home Cats pretending to be the invading army of Outling Cats were all ranged on the far side of the wild grassy area with the tangle of trees and

7

bushes behind them. Dorothy said it would look like they'd burst through the undergrowth to attack. I noticed the three Spartacii crouching low, ready to spring forward. Ginger sat placidly behind them, like a furry marmalade coloured wall of muscle.

She turned to the other Home Cats. 'Remember to follow Spartacus,' I heard her say.

'Which one?' someone called out from the back.

'Me!' said the rangy fellow with the cleft chin.

'No, me! *I'm* Spartacus!' declared the Red Point Siamese indignantly.

'Oh, don't start *that* again!' sighed Ginger, before the third Spartacus could answer.

On our side of the grass, the Allotment defenders were placed. Red Fred, Dorothy and I were defending cats – Dorothy was, of course, going to lead the charge, filming as she did so – and we would be followed by the combined ranks of stoats, weasels, foxes, badgers and hedgehogs and, of course, Rosie. A couple of hares had just joined us, so each of these were placed on opposite sides of the defenders as Elite Attackers, as Dorothy called them.

Meanwhile, ET would be filming from one side of the action, held steady by Barbara (who was staying out of Dorothy's way), G.G. would be filming from the other side and Janet would be filming looking down at the action from Up a tree. Red Fred and I looked up at her now, as she inched out along an overhanging branch to get the best vantage point.

'I think Janet's in the safest place,' I muttered to Fred.

'I think you could be right, mate,' said Fred. He nodded to the "Outling Invaders" across the way from us. 'I haven't play-wrestled with Ginger since we were kittens. She looks pretty tough now, don't she?'

'At least you know her,' I replied. 'Some of those Home Cats chased me out of their gardens when I was an Outling, I always used to throw insults at them when I legged it. I think they want to get even.'

'Don't you worry Rob mate,' said Red Fred, giving me a friendly nudge which nearly knocked me over. 'If anyone makes it too real with you, I'll flatten 'em! You Stand By Me.'

'Thanks Fred,' I said gratefully. 'Mind you, I don't like the way the stoats and weasels are winding the badgers up much either.'

We looked around at the stoats and weasels who were jabbering to each other deliberately loud so the badgers could hear them:

'I've heard of that book *Windy Willies* where the Badger beats up the stoats and weasels!'

'*Yeah right!* Only 'cos 'e got a mole an' a rat an' a toad to 'elp 'im though, didn't 'e?'

'Don't like toads – they taste 'orrible. I wouldn't try on that Tiberius toad either, 'Es got magic, e' has!'

'Tiberius ain't in this book. I mean – film…'

'I wouldn't reckon a mole could do much anyway – they can't see unless they're underground!'

'Rats don't get involved.'

''E was a water vole anyway, wasn't 'e?'

'Who was?'

'The rat in the *Wind up your Willies* book!'

'Badgers! They reckon they're *sooooo* tough!'

One of the badgers shouted back: 'We can hear you, you know! We're *supposed* to be on the same
de!'

The stoats and weasels all started chanting, taunting the badgers: *'Come on if you think you're 'ard
ough!'* *'You're goin' home in an ambulance!'* *'Who are Ya? Who are Ya?'*

The biggest badger, Mr Brock growled menacingly; *'Right!* You wait you slinky slimeballs – just
ou wait…'

'Uh-oh' muttered Red Fred ominously. 'There Will Be Blood… Have you seen those badgers'
ws?'

A group of rabbits hopped up to us, looking rather worried. The biggest rabbit with a shock of
fty fur on his head – obviously their leader - whispered to us conspiratorially: 'I don't think those
oats and weasels are interested in the movie at all. I think they're having their own private war with
e badgers.'

'Work that out all on your own, did you?' said Red Fred, with a hint of sarcasm. The rabbit
emed oblivious to this and rallied his group of bunnies to a position under a Hazel tree, just to the
ght of us.

'Who is *he* anyway?' I asked Fred.

'I bet you a Fiver he's one of their Bigwigs,' said Fred, knowingly.

'*If* you've all quite finished?' shouted Dorothy, in an attempt to get everyone's attention. 'When I
out "Action!" we all charge towards each other and pretend to fight. Those of you with collar
meras, film as you go and try and get some good close ups. Everybody ready?'

'*YERRRRRS*!' we all chorused.

'Okay then,' shouted Dorothy. 'Lights! Camera! *Action…!*'

CHAPTER SEVEN

And… Cut!

'I think *that* could have gone better,' I muttered groggily, as I slowly got to my feet, shaking the dust and grass off my coat. 'Talk about Mission Impossible…'

'You think?' mumbled Barbara, somewhat sarcastically I felt. Then again, he was stuck head-first in a bush, whilst Red Fred tried to pull him out by locking his big claws on Barbara's hips and tugging. Suddenly, with a rustling, twiggy kind of plop, Barbara came free from the bush and he and Fred tumbled backwards onto the grass. Barbara sat up, shaking leaves and bits of twig out of his ears and whiskers. His fur was sticking out at odd angles. I knew it would take him hours to wash that flat.

'The badgers certainly gave those stoats and weasels what for, didn't they?' chuckled Red Fred.

Judging by the number of walloped weasels and semi-conscious stoats lying around, I had to agree with his assessment.

As I'd observed many times previously, nothing ever seemed to bother Red Fred. Then again, he hadn't been stampeded over by three fox cubs, four home cats and a Rosie.

'Reckon we got some good footage then?' mused Fred, adjusting his KittyCam™ collar. 'I had quite a few Close Encounters.'

'Hope so, Brother Dear,' said Ginger as she strolled over, nudging a stunned stoat out of her way with her Left Foot. 'Did you see me and that hare go at it? He came lolloping up to me, he did, stood on his hind legs waving his front paws at me and said… what was it now? Oh yes: "Put yer dukes up, Pussycat or get out of my way!"'

'Cheeky so-and-so! What did you say?' asked Fred.

Ginger grinned. 'I said to him: "You shall not pass!" Then I flattened him.'

'Hello there, are you all okay?' came a small, sympathetic voice. Janet slipped through the long grass to join us. She didn't have a hair out of place. She was followed a few seconds later by E.T. who tumbled and crashed through the grass in her usual crab-walk fashion.

'I-I-I- I think *Igotsomegreat* action shots!' wibbled E.T. 'Well, I did u-u-until a hedgehog fell on *Barbaraandknockedhimover*, then *I* r-r-rolled *downtheslope* to the pond. I th-th-think I ended f-f-*ilmingaloadof* tadpoles.'

'A hedgehog *fell* on you?' I said, incredulously.

'It's true!' exclaimed Barbara. 'E.T.'s my Witness! An owl did it. It picked up a hedgehog and dropped it on my head! *An owl. Dropped a hedgehog. On my head!* Blooming prickly it was too!'

'I didn't know we had any owls taking part in the movie,' I said. 'I know the crows were on standby for some aerial action…'

'And *I* saw that foreign eagle thing swooping down as well,' grumbled Barbara. 'The one that flew in from the sunny south just recently.'

'O-o-oh, *youmean* The Maltese Falcon?' wibbled E.T. 'I-I-I d-d-did *seeanowlaswell*. One Flew Over the Cuckoo's Nest. W-w-well it's a thrush's nest r-r-really, b-b-but there's a cuckoo ch-ch-*chickinitnow.*'

'It all looked a bit violent from where I was filming up the tree,' added Janet. 'I thought you were supposed to be *pretending* to fight?'

'*We* thought so too!' muttered Barbara.

Just at that moment Rosie came bounding over, tongue lolling. 'Wasn't that *fun?*' she yapped cheerfully. 'Oh, I chased *loads* of those Home Cats *right* out of the allotments! Wasn't I supposed to do that? Oh well, they needed to go home anyway. Ah yes, that's what I came to say. My human is ready to go now and she's calling me, so I'd better be off. Thanks for letting me play with you all! I really enjoyed myself! What a Dog Day Afternoon I've had! It's a Dog's Life! See you later! Bye!' With that she bowled me over with an enthusiastic lick and then scooted away through the grass towards the allotments.

'It's been The Longest Day. I think I need a lie down after all this,' I said. 'Come on, let's go to the Clubhouse.'

'And I need to get back home too,' said Ginger. 'Hope you got enough film, Bro, 'cos I don't think I'll be able to persuade any of my moggy mates to come back for more. They prefer life on Easy Street.'

'I'll walk you to the gate, Sis,' said Red Fred. 'Thanks for sorting this anyway. I must try out that move you made on me sometime.'

'Which one?' asked Ginger as they strolled away.

'The one where you jumped up and down on my head. I'm not Unbreakable, you know.'

As we strolled onto the allotments, we saw the three Spartacii weaving from side to side, holding each other up as they did so. It looked like they'd seen quite a bit of fight action.

'Let's go home,' I heard the black and white one say. 'I don't think I'm cut out for a movie career.'

'Me neither,' said the Red Point Siamese. 'I could've been a contender, but, well, maybe not. I'm just not The Wild One.'

'My name's not really Spartacus anyway,' added the rangy fellow with the cleft chin. 'It's Kirk.'

'I'm not really Spartacus either,' admitted the black and white boy. 'I'm Oscar. I just liked the sound of Spartacus.' They both stopped, turned and looked at the Siamese, questioningly.

'Me? I really *am* Spartacus!' he insisted.

'I thought your name was Giles!'

'No, I'm *Spartacus*!'

'No, you're not!'

'It's the truth I tell you!'

'Liar! Liar!'

'I tell you – it's the truth! You can't handle the truth!'

'Well, in that case, *I'm* Spartacus!'

'No, *I'm* Spartacus!'

We walked around them and left them to it. They obviously had a bad case of artistic
mperament.

On our way back to the clubhouse, we found Dorothy in one of the recently seeded plots, lying on
er back with her legs in the air. I didn't think the plot holder would be very pleased if she'd squashed
s seedlings.

'Dorothy? Chief? Are you – are you alright?' I asked with genuine concern.

I was relieved when Dorothy slowly rolled over onto her side. I noticed a few muddy pawprints on
er coat, a combination of cat, fox and hare by the looks of things. 'Oh, hello,' said Dorothy dreamily,
ith a faraway look in her eyes.

'Are you sure you're okay?' I added, with concern. 'I wouldn't worry about the battle scene, I
1ow it could have been better but…'

Dorothy didn't seem to hear me. 'It was *brilliant!*' she enthused, a sudden manic gleam coming
to her eyes. 'Great action scenes! Terrific battle sequences! G.G. is going to have great fun when
1e uploads the film to the laptop. It's going to be *epic!*'

'So - er – you're happy with how it went then?' asked Janet. 'You know, what with being trampled
1 and all? I saw that happen from the tree. I think I got footage of it…'

'A good actor and director suffers for their art,' declared Dorothy, dramatically. 'Anyway, until
morrow team! *Cut!*'

'And a bruise or two,' I added, with feeling.

CHAPTER EIGHT

Close Up

We filmed over the next three days and nights. Dorothy was relentless in what she called "the pursuit of her artistic vision". Perhaps wisely, she'd given up trying to direct every scene herself and had - somewhat reluctantly – given Barbara the task of being Assistant Director. I figured she must have calmed down after her outburst at Barbara on the first day.

I actually thought it was quite clever how she had worked things out. She outlined what was to be filmed, who was to do and say what and then told Barbara to take whichever of us he needed (assuming Dorothy didn't need us for a scene she was filming) and to go and film it somewhere else. I felt that maybe it was just an excuse to get Barbara out of her way.

It turned out that working with Barbara as Director was a lot easier than working with Dorothy. For a start, Barbara didn't shout and get angry, which was a bonus. He appointed a young hedgehog named Hannah to be *his* assistant and to make sure we all "hit our marks" (I never did find anyone called Mark to hit) and act out what we were pretending to do. Hannah had made Barbara's acquaintance after being dropped on his head during the battle scene. Barbara didn't hold it against Hannah, who hadn't expected to be flying at that point anyway, which made us question the owl's motivation in the first place. She proved herself to be a very eager and cheerful little hedgehog, despite having to film in daytime and kept us all laughing with her funny quips about how our segments of the completed movie would be so much better than Dorothy's. 'That's because it's a Barbara and Hannah production!' she said.

'I think a Hannah Barbara production sounds better,' said Barbara generously. 'This is the beginning of beautiful friendship.'

Anyway, we simply got on with our scenes, which were mainly "close ups", where us actors would be talking or reacting to something.

I was dozing happily on a log when I heard my name being called by Hannah. I yawned, stretched and then jumped off the log to make my way to the patch of wild area where we were filming. 'I'm ready for my close up.' I said breezily as I trotted onto set.

'Jolly good!' said Barbara. 'Now, Janet here will be filming your reaction to the big fight that's going on…'

'Where?' I said looking around, startled. 'I can't see any fight.'

Barbara sighed. 'No, I know there isn't,' he said patiently. 'Dorothy is still filming that. *This* little bit will be a close-up shot of you looking on in surprise as the invaders swarm onto the allotments. This bit of film will be added to the fight scene later, see?'

I didn't, but I nodded anyway.

'Then, you're going to be the hero of the hour!' continued Barbara. 'You have to narrow your eyes, jut your chin out with determination, look about to the other cats – yes, I know there aren't any here, but pretend they are, ok? Then you shout: "We must defend our allotments! Charge! No prisoners! No prisoners!"'. You got that?'

'I'm the hero?' I gasped. 'Wow!' I thought back to the filming of the fight scene a few days ago. I hadn't felt that heroic then.

'Well, you *did* rally us all against those humans who tried to burn down the allotments,' said Janet looking down shyly. I thought how pretty her fur looked when it caught the sunlight, showing up patches of coppery orange and subtle tabby grey.

'*Ooh yes*!' squealed Hannah, excitedly, snapping my attention back to the film. 'I Know What You Did Last Summer! I was just a little nailbrush at the time, but I remember that big meeting all the animals were at, by the pond. Then the next night Mum and Dad and the other big Hogs went off to fight the bad humans. They said you were brilliant Robert, giving orders and getting everybody where they needed to be!'

I didn't *quite* remember it like that, but then Janet had told me later that real heroes were always modest. Besides, she added, the real Battle of the Allotments was recounted in my book and everybody who read it knew that I was the hero. I remembered that afterwards, even Dorothy had been quite... well, *nice* to me, at least for a while. I had a vision of me as the handsome hero and Dorothy as my adoring heroine. I tilted my chin in what I hoped was a heroic pose. 'Let's do this thing!' I said decisively.

It was another night of filming. The allotments are different at night. Obviously, it's darker, but it has a beauty all its own and when it comes down to it, they're not much different than during daytime. We cats can see somewhat better than humans in the dark, so the colours of the flowers and vegetables change subtly into different shades. Most flowers close their petals at night, but even then, they glow for us. Then of course you get all the different insects and small creatures that you don't see during the day, scuttling and slithering about, making their own noises, conversing with each other in their own strange, clicking, shuffling and sinuous languages. Moths flutter by, chasing their wafting, winding scent trails. I'm sure they deliberately dip low to tease us cats and get us to swipe at them. Most of the time they flit off, but other times they're not so lucky. Mind you, there's not a lot you can do with them once you catch them - moths taste very dusty and bitter. I prefer crane flies, they're nice and crunchy, although there's not much meat on them.

Usually, I'd be out and about looking for mice or voles to chase and occasionally catch and eat as they busily forage for seeds and fallen fruits or insects, always being careful not to collide with an owl that's after the same mouse or vole. Red Fred said that happened to him once. He and the owl ended up nutting each other silly and the mouse they were after got away. Oh, and don't believe this human idea that owls are wise and all-knowing. Never try talking to an owl – they just ignore you. Basically, they couldn't give a hoot.

Barbara, naturally, was particularly wary of owls after his recent experience.

Dorothy was in charge tonight and assured us that this was the very last bit of filming we needed to do. It was to be mainly shots of us running in and out of the various plots in the allotment, as we headed to the grassy wild area to make our stand against the invaders the following day.

The first night we'd filmed had been fine. The day had been warm and sunny, the night was still warm and pleasant. But the temperature had dropped tonight. Maybe it's just as well we would be running. Although I had to say I preferred filming In The Heat of the Night.

'Can we hurry it up?' I grumbled. 'I'm Frozen!'

'I'm Frozen Too,' added Dorothy, 'But I'm making this sacrifice for my art! And I'm doing this all on my own because G.G. is in the clubhouse editing the footage we've already shot, so I'm working without an assistant tonight.'

'I'll be your assistant, Chief!' squeaked Hannah excitedly hurrying over to Dorothy.

'Who are you, then?' said Dorothy, peering down at the little hedgehog.

'Say hello to my little friend,' said Barbara. 'This is Hannah, she's a great assistant.'

'Hmm, well, okay, said Dorothy, dubiously. 'Just make sure everything goes according to plan and that everyone is where they're supposed to be.'

'You got it, Chief!' enthused Hannah. 'It's a great honour to be working with you. Oh, The Prestige.'

Despite the cold, we made good progress that night. Dorothy had plenty of close-up shots of us cats emerging from the foliage on the plots. I was filmed sneaking round the Chicken Run. I managed to do this very quietly without waking any of the hens, which was a bonus.

Eventually, Dorothy was happy with everything. We were all flagging, although Hannah still seemed pretty lively. Then again, she had snacked on lots of slugs during the night, which of course we couldn't do, although to her credit, she very politely offered us some.

Dorothy called us all to attention. 'Well done team!' she said proudly. 'You've all worked quite hard to help create my movie. It's going to be brilliant! You're all invited to the world premier this weekend when the movie is released online! Humans and pets will be talking about it all over The Social Network!'

We all gave a ragged cheer.

'I know It's Been A Hard Day's Night,' added Dorothy. 'But we finished filming just Before Sunrise!'

'She loves the Spotlight, doesn't she?' muttered Barbara to me.

'I think A Star Is Born.' I chuckled.

It was with a collective sigh of relief that we heard Dorothy bring the movie filming to a close. 'Okay Cat People… That's a Wrap!'

CHAPTER NINE

World Premier!

It was Sunday afternoon. Betty had gone home for a few hours and no other humans were in the clubhouse, so all of us Allotment cats were gathered there, crowded round Betty's laptop. G.G. had nudged the laptop into the middle of the desk to give us all room to sit on the desk or stand up on the chairs with our front paws in the desk so we could see the screen.

None of us, apart from Dorothy, had seen G.G. for days. According to Dorothy G.G. had been sleeping most of the days and then "pulling all-nighters" to upload the footage from our KittyKam™ collars onto the memory-stick-control-thingy and from there onto the laptop, where she would do her eddying to put the film together. G.G. had told us that the correct term was editing, but Dorothy did that all the time – she'd often smack my head, so what head hitting had to do with anything I wasn't sure. Then again, I didn't pretend that I knew much about making movies. Dorothy had popped in several times to supervise (or Poke Her Nose In as Red Fred had put it), but had largely left things to G.G.

I had to say, G.G. looked very tired that afternoon. But at the same time she looked excited.

'How did you get into the clubhouse at night, G.G.?' I asked.

'Through the Rear Window,' replied G.G. 'It doesn't close properly, so I just nose it up, slip through and then it drops down behind me, just like one of our cat flaps.' She chuckled to herself. 'A couple of times I've worked so hard I've fallen asleep in the clubhouse, but when I've heard Betty's car pull up, and I haven't had time to make a Great Escape and scramble out of the window, I just hide. Betty always leaves the door open for us, so when she's not looking, I scoot up to the door and then walk in, so she thinks I've come in from the allotments. So, Betty gives me some breakfast and then I trot off to my human's shed and sleep some more.'

'Th-th-that *rearwindowis* v-v-very high up,' observed E.T. 'I c-c-couldn't *getupthere*. I-I-I'd get vertigo.'

'I just couldn't fit through it anyway,' chuckled Red Fred. 'I'd get Stuck.'

'You've done very well G.G.,' conceded Dorothy. She turned to look at us all. 'In fact, I'd say you've all done *fairly* well, so thank you for that. I think my movie will...'

'*Our* movie, Princess,' corrected Red Fred.

'Er... yes... *our* movie will receive wide acclaim,' continued Dorothy. 'It should cheer everybody up in these worrying times.'

We all voiced our agreement. There were still very few humans visiting the allotments and they were still keeping apart – soshul dissing I think they called it. G.G. added that the Lockdown was still in progress and that the virus was still causing many more deaths and all the problems that went with it.

'I saw Rosie this morning,' I said. 'She told me that young Tom is still in hospital and misses everybody. He talks to his sister Amelia on his tabby-let most days and one of the nurses has put a laptop on the ward for the kids to see films and things on, but it still gets quite boring, so he'd love to see Rosie in the movie.'

'Well, I think he might be very pleased then,' said Dorothy proudly. 'G.G.…. are you ready to show us the finished movie?'

'Ready to roll, Chief!' purred G.G., flicking her claws across the laptop keys. She directed the cursor to a square folder icon marked Movie. 'Here we go!' she declared.

The folder opened to a greeny-blue screen on which in bold red letters were written a number of words. G.G. read them out to us:

tHe BAtTeL 4 SUnNySyDe ALLotMenTs

WriTed bY, dIrEctEd an STarRiNg

DoRoTHy DuM pLinG, C.A.T.

Wiv ROBeRt and EvRyOnE eLse

'Hmmm,' said Dorothy narrowing her eyes at the screen. 'I thought you said you could type, G.G. Those letters look a bit funny to me. Hard to read.'

'Oh, don't worry about that,' said G.G. quickly. 'Loads of humans type funny online and don't know how to spell words. They don't think it matters. They'll probably be able to read it better like this anyway.'

'Uh-huh,' muttered Dorothy. She peered close to the screen again. 'What does that say after my name?'

'Director!' said G.G. quickly. 'Never mind that - look, the movie's starting!'

'Oooh!' we all chorused and leaned forward as the movie began.

'As I told you Dorothy,' said G.G., 'There was quite a bit of footage that was too blurred or shaky to use, or someone would put their big paws over the camera lens…' She threw a glance at Red Fred. 'But I did the best I could with what was left.'

We watched, entranced, as we saw images of each of us trotting around the allotments or dozing in various places, like seed trays, vegetable plots, sheds and occasionally our cat beds. Then there was Rosie bounding across the screen towards the camera. She went all blurry then a big pink thing – her tongue I realised – covered the camera lens, then the picture kind of fell over and ended up showing the sky – a very blurry and wet sky.

'Ah yes, that was a bit you filmed, Robert,' said G.G.

There followed lots of snippets of other animals, hedgehogs, badgers, stoats and weasels (who were jumping up and down excitedly), then Ruby and her fox cubs running from one side of the screen to the other.

'There's no sound,' Dorothy said, flatly.

'Ah, well, the KittyKam™ collars don't have microphones, or if they do I couldn't work out how
 switch them on,' said G.G. 'But don't worry Dorothy, I thought of that. I've written some
 ubbertattles.'

As soon as she said that, I saw my handsome face on the screen, looking alert. My eyes narrowed
 nd my noble chin jutted, then the picture became words which G.G. read out as: *'We are under
 'tack!'*

There was a quick shot of Red Fred, then the picture changed to a shot from high up showing lots
 ' Home Cats walking along the grassy area.

'That's my bit from up the tree!' piped up Janet.

'Shhh!' Dorothy scolded her as the image changed to me in close-up again opening and closing my
 outh. Some more subbytattles came up, which G.G. read out as: *"We must defend our allotments!
 harge! No prisoners! No prisoners!"'*

Then the movie got really exciting as there were quick images of Fred and Ginger wrestling, the
 ree Spartacii cats leaping towards the camera, then lots of fairly shaky shots of different animals
 nning around. There was a particularly good shot of Mr Brock the badger barging into a gaggle of
 oats and weasels, sending them flying. It all got a bit confusing after that, especially where the
 mera appeared to be rolling down a hill and then ended up in the water, with a lot of tadpoles
 vimming past in confusion.

'Th-th-that's *mybitthatis*!' wibbled E.T. excitedly and nearly fell off the desk. Thankfully Red Fred
 eadied her with his paw.

Suddenly Dorothy appeared on the screen in close-up, obviously yelling. It was quite disconcerting
 nd made us all jump back in alarm, even Dorothy herself.

Finally, there was a long shot of Rosie chasing half a dozen Home Cats through the allotments,
 oviously thoroughly enjoying herself.

Then the screen turned bluey-green again and two words appeared:

ThE End

The movie stopped. Nobody said a word. It was so quiet we could hear the clubhouse clock
 :king. In fact, you could have heard a hedgehog drop. We all glanced nervously at Dorothy who was
 ll staring at the screen, as though she could see something we couldn't see. One by one we began to
 ealthily edge away and climb down from the desk and chairs. Only G.G. remained where she was
 oking from Dorothy to the screen and back again. We were heading towards the door, fully
 pecting to hear an eruption of hissing, spitting and swearing when Dorothy spoke, very quietly.

'Not bad. Not bad at all.'

G.G. let out a long gasp, having been holding her breath.

Dorothy stood up, arched her back and stood on her toes in a good, long stretch, then sat down
 ain and started to wash her face, dabbing behind her ears with her paws. We all hurried back to the
 sk and congratulated her.

'Brilliant work, Princess!'

'That's a blockbuster that is!'

'Everyone will say what a great director you are!'

'Human and animals will love it!'

'I l-l-liked *thetadpoles!*'

Dorothy modestly accepted our praise, then turned to G.G. 'Great editing G.G.,' she said. 'So… shall we put it out there?'

'Where?' I asked.

Dorothy gave me a Look. 'Online, Dopey!' she said.

G.G. quickly tapped some keys and then sat back. She pointed to a big key. 'Press Send, Chief,' she smiled. 'That'll put it online. I can upload it to Robert's *Nitter-Natter* and *FaceyFriend* pages.'

'Isn't the Interweb great?' said Barbara. 'We certainly live in Modern Times.'

Dorothy extended her paw and then flicked a claw out and tapped the key. We all cheered, at a job well done. Then we all decided that the best thing to do was to go and catch some late afternoon sunshine. Dorothy proudly led us out into the allotments, her tail high in the air.

'What did you do with the footage left over, G.G.?' she asked casually.

'I – er – I think I put them in the Recycle Bin on the laptop,' said G.G.

'Oh,' said Dorothy. Then she added brightly: 'If they're still there, save them. We can always issue a Director's Cut later.'

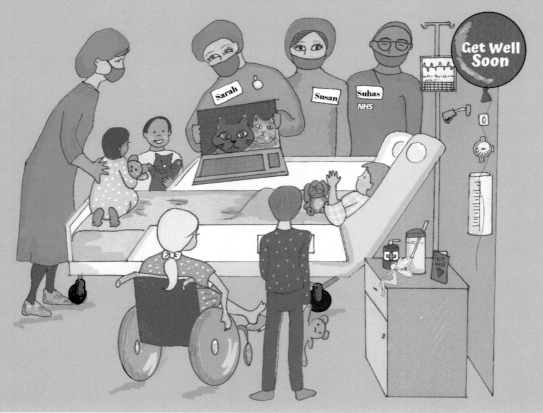

CHAPTER TEN

Critical Acclaim

The movie was very well received. Betty was soon spending hours on the laptop sending messages and replying to emails and posting messages "from me" on my *Nitter-Natter* and *FaceyFriends* pages. The other allotment holders had all been calling to congratulate Betty, who in turn was asking which of them had put the footage together, which everyone denied. Tom's mum and dad said that he had watched it on the nurse's laptop in hospital over and over again and was proudly telling all the other children in the ward that Rosie was his dog, also that was the allotments where his family had a plot. It had cheered him up no end, which was what we wanted of course.

G.G. read some of the messages out to us one day when Betty was off home. Lots of the local Home Cat's humans had identified their cats in the movie and had posted messages saying they had no idea that they went over to the allotments. One particular exchange made me chuckle:

'I'm sure that's my Spartacus.'

'No, that's my *Spartacus.'*

'I thought your cat was called Kurt.'

'No, that's Oscar, surely?'

'Look, I know my *cat. Your cat is Giles. I know this, because he's always in my garden.* My *cat is Spartacus.'*

'You're both wrong. My *cat is Spartacus!'*

After this, the moderator (whatever that is) had blocked further comments on that thread.

Apparently, the movie had been viewed millions of times around the world. Newspapers, TV and Online Meejah people were messaging Betty all the time. If they weren't interviewing her via the laptop on video messaging, they were on the phone to her. In fact, it was strange to see her without her phone pressed against her ear.

Of course, Betty kept telling everyone who asked that she had no idea who had put the film together. The standard response to this was *'Well, the cats did it of course eh? Ha! Ha!'* The documentary makers were apparently delighted that the KittyCam™ collars had produced such great images. I was lying on Betty's desk one day and listened in to a video conversation between Betty and the Director of the documentary. He was an odd looking human with a beard, who wore his baseball cap on backwards.

'Hi Mrs DeGatto! It's Ridley Quentin Lucasberg here, from True to Life Films. How're you doing? Staying safe, I hope? Oh Mrs DeGatto, it was so fortunate that you turned the cameras on. Otherwise we wouldn't have seen all those great images,' he enthused. 'Robert has got to be the most famous cat on the planet. He looks like a noble Black Panther!'

'But Mr Lucasberg, I really don't remember turning the collars on, apart from that one time when I tested Dorothy's camera,' said Betty, a little flustered. 'I must've nudged the control thingy by mistake.'

'Ah, not to worry,' said the Director dismissively. 'Mistakes like that are fine! It's all great publicity for the documentary when we get around to filming it, once this terrible virus is behind us. The manufacturers of the collars are delighted too – apparently people are wanting KittyKam™ collars for their cats, dogs, rabbits, you name it. One lady even put in an order for some small collars for her pet Fancy Rats! They're making hundreds of collars as we speak. We're going to do a deal with them on showing the "movie"…,' Here he waggled his fingers in the air for some reason, before continuing. 'We'll get a percentage of the profits as will the Allotment Cats Veterinary Fund and any charity you want to name. Assuming you're agreeable to us using the footage, of course.'

They talked about money for a while after that and I dozed off. I may have mentioned before I have no idea about this money thing that humans use so much. I woke up again just as the conversation was finishing.

'Well, goodbye Mrs DeGatto, and thanks again,' said the Director cheerfully. 'By the way, do you know what someone called the movie? No? They called it *"The Viral Hit to Beat the Virus Blues."* Isn't that great?'

Betty agreed that it was. She still looked bemused though. She clicked the laptop screen off as the conversation ended and then looked over at me. 'Did *you* make this movie, Robert?' she asked with a smile. 'Or did Dorothy?'

I yawned, stretched and answered: 'We *all* did. Just call us The Magnificent Seven.'

Of course, all she heard was '*Miaow, miaow, miaow,*' which usually means '*I want some cat treats*'. So, she obligingly got up and fetched some for me.

'Well Robert, how does it feel to be a movie star?' Janet asked me, 28 Days Later, as we patrolled the allotments. It had been a lovely sunny warm day and the sun was just beginning to sink on the horizon, painting the sky and few clouds in vivid shades of orange, red and purple 'You're not just a Local Hero, you know. You're Notorious.'

'What does that mean?' I asked.

'Famous, I think. People are saying you're a National Treasure. Once the Lockdown's over, you'll probably get invited with Betty to go on TV down in the Metropolis.'

'That sounds good.'

'Of course,' Janet added, 'Dorothy's been saying that she's the *real* star of the movie.'

'Well, I won't fight her about it,' I sighed. 'We don't want any Star Wars on the allotments.'

'You know her Inside Out, don't you?' giggled Janet. 'If you steal her limelight, I've got a Sixth Sense you'd be Unforgiven.'

'Ah, it's not in my nature to push myself forward or become a Raging Bull,' I said. 'I'm happy being a Camera Person. In fact, I'm just happy being an Allotment Cat.'

'Me too,' agreed Janet.

We both sat and looked at the sky and it deepened from dark red, to purple-black.

'Let's hope this awful virus passes soon,' I said. 'Things will get back to normal. I know people are fed up being cooped up at home, not being able to visit their family and friends. But it could be worse.'

'That's right,' agreed Janet. 'I used to be someone's pet once, before my owner passed away. If they've got pets, they'll be a great comfort to them right now. Things can always be worse.'

We rubbed noses. A bat flew past, hurrying to catch insects on the wing. An owl hooted from the wild side. I heard Ruby's cubs barking in their throaty foxy way. A hedgehog rustled and snuffled by through some fallen leaves.

I purred contentedly and said: 'It's a Wonderful Life.'

THE END

End Credits

To say we live in challenging and scary times is an understatement right now. The global pandemic of the Coronavirus Covid-19 has literally shaken our everyday life to its very foundations.

Many of us will have lost friends and relatives to this deadly virus which makes no distinction in its victims; rich or poor, young or old. Governments the world over have introduced Lockdowns to ensure that people stay at home to stay healthy. Sports arenas, offices, factories, schools, cinemas, theatres, children's playgrounds, non-essential shops are all closed. Many people, classed as highly vulnerable due to pre-existing medical conditions, or by the medication that they are taking, or by disability and so on have even greater restrictions placed on their freedom. This includes Yours Truly and Tom, my brilliant illustrator Bex's 8-year old son.

I'll let Bex explain more about Tom's condition on the next page, but she highlights a very important group of people to whom we should all be grateful at this time: *Our Healthcare Professionals*. Wherever in the world you live, we should all be immensely grateful to these dedicated, caring people; Doctors, Nurses, Consultants, Radiologists, Nursing Assistants, Phlebotomists and so many more, including a whole army of support staff from Cleaners to Porters to Administrators and everybody inbetween.

And of course, there's all our *Frontline Workers* too who are keeping everything going: Mental Health and Learning Disability Professionals, Home Carers, Care Home Staff, Shop Assistants, Delivery people, Dustmen, Bus Drivers, Train Drivers, Tram Drivers, Taxi Drivers, Lorry Drivers… the list goes on and on. As well as thousands of volunteers……

So yes – challenging and scary times indeed.

But…

… It's important to be optimistic; these times *will* pass. The world *will* go back to something approaching normality, and we *will* be able to lead our daily lives again at work and play. In the meantime though, it's equally important to be happy and find fun wherever you can. This short story in the *Robert The Allotment Cat* series is our way – that's Robert, his fellow Allotment Cats, Bex and me – of bringing a bit of humour and fun to proceedings. Also, we hope to raise a bit of money for the Evelina Children's Hospital, to help support those healthcare professionals to whom we owe so much. Because they're *there for us,* not just during the Coronavirus pandemic, but always.

And where would we be without them?

Stay Safe, Stay Well, Keep Smiling… and Thank You.

Nick, Bex and Robert & co.
April 2020

PS: If you can spot all the film titles and quotes in this silly story, well, that's all part of the fun. Me? I lost count!

A Word From Bex

ur son Tom is a kind and thoughtful eight-year old boy; he loves science, playing with his sister Amelia, his ts, Fluffy and Zoom but his biggest love in the whole word is his bouncy dog, Rosie.

wo years ago, just before Tom turned 6, he became seriously ill with a rare neurological illness. Over the last vo years Tom has spent long periods of time in hospital. Tom is currently being treated by the **Evelina hildren's Hospital** for neuro inflammatory syndrome and a brain tumour, he will remain in their care for the st of his childhood.

/e continue to be immensely grateful to all the hospital staff for their generosity of time, care and love that they ow Tom on a daily basis. To thank them we are raising money to help them to continue to give specialist care the most critically ill children and hope to their families.

you would like to donate to The Evelina Children's hospital then you can do so by going www.justgiving.com/Rebecca-Homewood1

osie especially would be enormously grateful as she hates it when Tom is away from home in hospital.

hank You.

ebecca "Bex" Homewood
pril 2020

It's The End… of *Robert The Movie Star,*
but Robert **will** return in…

Robert The Allotment Cat:
A Winter's Tail

Printed in Great Britain
by Amazon

81911216R00031